Light +
Dark

Full Moon
Barnyard Dance

To Waldo, my full moon partner,
and to the Reed and Tacquard clans, whose mix is fun
enough for many a barnyard dance
– C. L. S.

Full Moon Barnyard Dance

CAROLE LEXA SCHAEFER

illustrated by

CHRISTINE DAVENIER

WALKER BOOKS
AND SUBSIDIARIES
LONDON • BOSTON • SYDNEY

Once, on a night with a bright full moon,
the barnyard animals just could *not* settle down.
With twitchy ears they listened to the
crickets' sweet night tunes, *zweet-zweet-zweet* . . .

and to Frog's deep bass music,
thrum, thrum, thrum.

"What a moo-oon," crooned
the cow beside the barn.

"Maa-agnificent night,"
bleated a goat in the grass.

"Good for a snufflin' big dance,"
snorted a pig in the mud.

"Down by the pond," clucked
the hens from their nests.

"Right nee-ow," sang the cats   on the wall. "Nee-oww."

Two by two, the animals left the barnyard.

Cow and bull ambled. Goats pranced.
Pigs trotted. Roosters and hens scurried.
And the cats – they sashayed all the way to the pond.

There, by the light of the bright round moon,
cow and bull danced triple-step dips.

Goats together
billy-bobbed the bebop.

Pig pairs wibbled their very own jigs.

Hens and roosters flapped
a fancy fandango.

And the cats – they
slink-slanked the samba.

But then, from the south – *reeoosh!* –
a rowdy wind blew in a crowd
of bumptious clouds.
They shut the moonlight out.
In the deep, deep dark, the crickets,
zweet-zweet-zweet, and Frog,
thrum, thrum, thrum, sang on.

So, with a shrug, and a twirl,
and a swing, swirl, swing,
the barnyard animals kept dancing.

In the dark, dark night, the bull murmured to the cow,
"My dear, did you say 'moo' or 'miaow'?"

A rooster whispered,
"Hen, dearest, your beak feels
soft as Piggy's snout."

The stoutest pig squealed, "Why, Mr Hog, tonight
you're dancing frisky as a kid!"

Then, from the north – *shareesh!* – a swift wind
whisked the bumptious clouds away.
The animals danced in
moonlight again.

But when, two by two they looked at each other – oh dear, what a mix-up! What a tangle! What a muddle!

"You are not my partner," each one cried.

From the middle of the pond came
a deep *thrum, thrum*. Frog in his big voice
sang, "Twirl, swirl again – don't stop so soon.
Do some *new* partner dancing, by the light of the moon."

And – step, stomp, shuffle, twirl, swing, swirl –
that is just what the barnyard animals did until . . .

they yawned and stretched and, two by two,
headed home to settle down at last.

"Huh," grunted the sleepy bull. "Tonight
I danced the samba with a cat. Rather nice."

"Mmph," mumbled a tired hen. "I jiggedy-jogged
with a hog. Very friendly."

"Most enjoyable," snuffled the stoutest pig,
"me, billy-bobbing with a kid."

Down by the pond, a cricket chirped.
"Do you think such a dance will ever
happen again?"

"Uhm-hmm. It'll keep coming round,"
thrummed Frog. He winked at the setting moon.
"Because everyone, mm-hmm, had fun."

First published 2003 by Walker Books Ltd
87 Vauxhall Walk, London SE11 5HJ

2 4 6 8 10 9 7 5 3 1

Text © 2003 Carole Lexa Schaefer
Illustrations © 2003 Christine Davenier

This book has been typeset in Kennerley

Printed in China

British Library Cataloguing in Publication Data:
a catalogue record for this book is available from the British Library

ISBN 0-7445-9339-5

www.walkerbooks.co.uk